BENEATH THE GHOST MOON

by Jane Yolen
Illustrated by Laurel Molk

Little, Brown and Company
Boston New York Toronto London

Text copyright © 1994 by Jane Yolen
Illustrations copyright © 1994 by Laurel Molk

First Edition

Library of Congress Cataloging-in-Publication Data

Yolen, Jane.
Beneath the ghost moon / by Jane Yolen ; illustrated by Laurel
Molk.
p.   cm.
Summary: Beneath the midnight moon, mice battle mean-hearted
creepy-crawlies to protect their farmyard home.
ISBN 0-316-96892-7
[1. Mice—Fiction. 2. Stories in rhyme.] I. Molk, Laurel, ill.
II. Title.
PZ8.3.Y76Be 1994
[E]—dc20   92-7625

54.982

10 9 8 7 6 5 4 3 2

NIL

Published simultaneously in Canada
by Little, Brown & Company (Canada) Limited

Printed in Italy

For Andrew Sigel—to boggle his mind
—J. Y.

To Jack Andrew Moldave
with all my love
—L. M.

'Twas the night before Ghost Eve,
And high in the sky,
The moon was an unblinking
Solid white eye.

The farmyard was quiet,
And likewise the house;
Asleep in each bed
Was a small, happy mouse.

Each dreamed of a dance
To a night-shining tune
Played under the stars
And the Halloween moon,

A fancy-dress dance
With a band that was hot
And a lemon-dew drink
Most decidedly not.

The costumes were gorgeous,
All fluffed, primped, and pressed,
With false nose or face mask
For each dancing guest.

And out in the garden patch
Under moon gleam,
The pumpkins all drowsed
In a vegetable dream.

But creeping from corners,
And creeping down walls,
And creeping from out of
Old dark cellar halls . . .

Came crimson and green things
That gibbered and laughed,
To steal all the face masks
And tear them in half.

They ripped up the costumes
While all the mice slept
(Except for one necklace,
A small crawly kept).

They trampled the noses,
And then—just for spite—
They dropped all the stuff
From a very great height.

They chortled their victory
Over the mice
And said lots of things
(Not a one of them nice).

Now one by one, waking,
The mice saw the mess:
The torn-apart face masks,
The ripped fancy dress.

They gathered the noses.
Not one was complete!
And everything soiled
By the creepy crew's feet.

All that was whole
In that terrible scene
Was a black clarinet
And a gold tambourine.

So one by one, crying,
They left the big house,
Every brown, every black,
Every gray or white mouse.

"It's the end!" cried a gray mouse.
"We're done!" wailed a black.
"Let us move far away
And let's never come back."

"Now, wait!" came a small voice.
"Don't give up so fast.
Please hear what I say
Before any vote's cast."

Then up on a pumpkin
So she could be seen,
Climbed a little white mouse
With the gold tambourine.

"Let us take back our home.
Let us take back the night.
We *can't* let that crew win
Without a good fight."

"But we're small." "And outnumbered!"
"It's just too much fuss!"
"Don't be daft," said the white mouse.
"What we've got is *us!*"

So they found rubber bands
And made slingshots of wood.
They gathered up all of the
Pebbles they could.

They fashioned pin swords
And made bottle-cap shields
And shaped cornstalk rammers
Picked up in the fields.

They took all the pull tabs
From soda-pop cans
And wore those as armor.
Then they made their plans.

"We'll stick them! We'll stalk them!
We'll make that crew sweat!"
Then a mouse blew a
C*H*A*R*G*E!
On the black clarinet.

They rushed through the darkness,
With banners held high,
And the farmyard hallooed
With a great battle cry.

The noise was quite wild
And quite deafening, too.
It certainly scared
That whole crawly-creep crew.

They fled from their lairs;
They dashed from their dens;
They stayed not a moment
To make their amends.

When last seen, the crawlies
Were headed due west.
"And that is the side of them
I like the best!"

The white mouse remarked,
And was turning around . . .

When there was her necklace
Strung out on the ground.

"Please, Miss," came a voice
With a hint of a whine,
"I am giving you back
What was yours, then was mine.

"Do you think I could stay
In your house (in my lair),
And be part of your home
And be part of your care?"

It was just a small crawlie,
A miserable creep,
And he ventured this question
Knees down in a heap.

"Stick him!" the mice cried.
The white mouse said, "No—
He has asked for our friendship.
We must let him go."

So they left him alone
In his dreadful distress.
And wearing their armor
Like Halloween dress,

They proceeded to dance
To a clarinet tune
And a tambourine beat
Underneath the Ghost Moon.

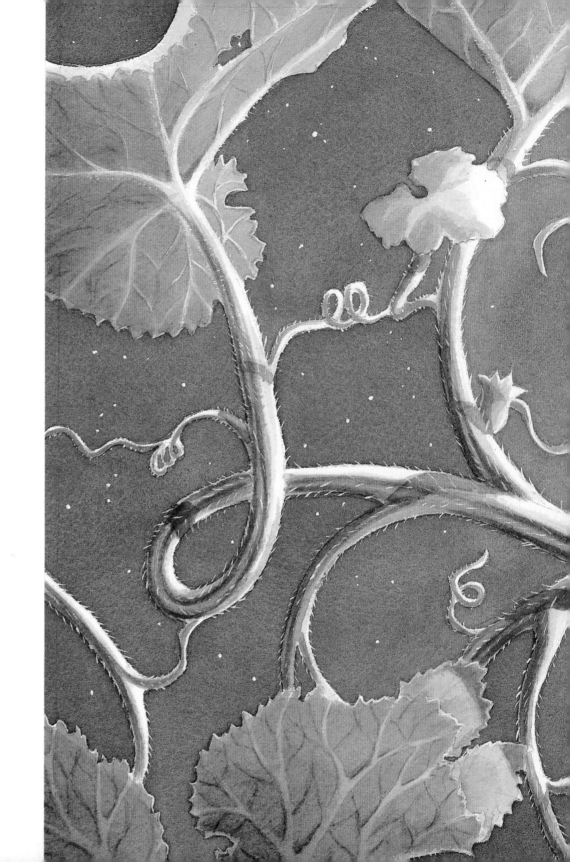

But off to one side,
With a tattered false nose,
In the soiled and torn remnants
Of some mouse's clothes,

The smallest of crawlies,
A smile on his face,
Got to listen to music
While dancing in place.

And when he was able
To follow the tune,
Why—

He danced with the white mouse
Beneath the Ghost Moon.

DATE DUE			
NO 13'96	SE 26'99	NO 04 02	
SE 28'96	OC 02'99		
OC 09'96	OC 07'99		
OC 17'96	OC 26'99		
NO 04'96	NO 09'99		
NO 18'96			
OC 14'97	OC 24'00		
OC 29'97	OC 30'00		
NO 06'97	OC 18'01		
OC 10'98	OC 31'01		
OC 19'98	SE 26'02		
NO 02'98	OC 08 02		